Leahann
the Birthday Present Fairy

To Emily Bartram, wishing you a magical future.

Special thanks to
Rachel Elliot

ORCHARD BOOKS

First published in Great Britain in 2023 by Hodder & Stoughton

1 3 5 7 9 10 8 6 4 2

© 2023 Rainbow Magic Limited.
© 2023 HIT Entertainment Limited.
Illustrations © 2023 Hodder & Stoughton Limited.

ISBN 978 140836 950 0

Printed and bound in Great Britain by Clays Ltd, Elcograf S.p.A.

Orchard Books
An imprint of Hachette Children's Group
Part of Hodder & Stoughton Limited
Carmelite House, 50 Victoria Embankment, London EC4Y 0DZ

An Hachette UK Company
www.hachette.co.uk
www.hachettechildrens.co.uk

Leahann
the Birthday Present Fairy

By Daisy Meadows

ORCHARD

www.orchardseriesbooks.co.uk

Jack Frost's Spell

The King and Queen are lazybones,
Sitting on their precious thrones.
King Oberon I'll overthrow,
And Queen Titania has to go.

Titania has a birthday law,
That helps her rule for decades more.
But I will freeze her gentle grace,
And set an Ice Queen in her place!

Contents

Chapter One
Partyland

"Rachel!"

Rachel Walker heard her best friend's voice before she saw her. Seconds later, Kirsty Tate ran up to Rachel and wrapped her in a big hug.

"Isn't this amazing?" Kirsty exclaimed.

The girls were at the Partyland

adventure park. It was their friend
Gracie Adebayo's birthday, and she was
celebrating on board the Partyland pirate
ship. They showed each other the gifts they
had bought.

"I couldn't wrap Gracie's present," said
Kirsty. "The sticky tape wouldn't hold and
the ribbon kept coming undone."

"I had the opposite," Rachel replied. "The
tape was so sticky that it ripped the paper,

and the ribbon wouldn't curl."

"I bet everyone had the same trouble wrapping their gifts," Kirsty went on. "And we know exactly why."

Rachel nodded, looking worried. "It's because Leahann's charm is still missing."

The girls had been friends with the fairies for a long time. They had shared many exciting adventures. Their new friends Gracie and Khadijah, were the only people who shared their wonderful secret.

A few days ago, Niamh the Invitation Fairy had come to invite them to Queen Titania's birthday party. But while she was there, Jack Frost had stolen four magical objects that belonged to Niamh and the rest of the Birthday Party Fairies. He and his sister, Jilly Chilly, wanted to rule Fairyland themselves.

Leahann

"This might be the most important magical adventure we've ever had," Rachel said. "If we don't find the last charm before Queen Titania's party, she might not be the queen any more."

There was going to be a very special ceremony at the Queen's birthday party. Every twenty years, she had to renew her right to be queen. If Jilly Chilly and Jack Frost had one of the charms, they could rule Fairyland.

"I hope that we can help Leahann," said Kirsty. "But right now, we need to find the pirate ship."

She looked up at a tall signpost beside them. It was filled with arrow-shaped signs pointed in all directions.

"Pirate ship straight ahead," said Rachel. "Let's go!"

They set off along a path of tiny white stones. It curved past the fairy tale forest, where a party of boys and girls were playing around a table filled with presents.

"Look at all the wrapping," said Kirsty.

The shiny paper was ripped and crumpled. Bows were flattened and ribbons hung limp.

"You see?" said Rachel with a sigh. "Every party here must have badly wrapped presents."

They turned a corner and forgot all about the presents. A brightly painted pirate ship was bobbing on a blue lake. Their friends Gracie and Khadijah were standing on the quarter deck.

"Rachel! Kirsty!" called Gracie, waving. "Come aboard!"

Rachel and Kirsty ran up the gangplank. At the same time, Gracie and Khadijah hurried down a steep ship's ladder to meet them. They all hugged.

"Happy birthday!" said Kirsty.

"I think this is the most perfect birthday I've ever had," said Gracie. "The pirate ship is amazing, every guest has arrived and we've got lots of party games to play."

"What's the first game?" Rachel asked.

Gracie smiled and clapped her hands together. "Treasure hunt!"

Rachel and Kirsty climbed up to the quarter deck and put their presents by the spokes of the ship's wheel. They noticed that most people had used bags without wrapping paper. Almost all the gifts seemed to be socks.

"Welcome, one and all!" boomed a deep voice.

A stubbly pirate was standing in the doorway of the room behind the ship's wheel. He had a large gold earring, a head scarf and a parrot on his shoulder.

"That's the party leader," Khadijah whispered, ducking behind Rachel. "Do you think he's a real pirate?"

"Gather round, me hearties," the party

leader rasped.

Gracie's guests gathered around him, and he lowered his voice to a whisper.

"Somewhere on board, there be a great treasure," he told them. "You have an hour to find it. Make groups of four. Each group will get different clues, but all will lead to the same treasure."

Rachel and Kirsty linked arms with Gracie and Khadijah. The pirate party leader gave them a scroll of ancient-looking paper, which they unrolled eagerly. The handwriting was thin and spiky, and the

paper was spattered with black ink.

Yo ho ho and a beard of red,
Where does the captain rest his head?
His trusty compass, round and old,
Will point you to the pirate gold.

Kirsty had the answer as quick as a flash.

"The captain's cabin, of course," she exclaimed.

"I know where that is," said Khadijah. "I saw it when I was exploring earlier."

She led them down the steep steps. They tiptoed through the pirates' sleeping area, where hammocks hung, swaying. A heavy wooden door was carved with the words:

Captain's Cabin

The door creaked as the girls opened it and stepped inside.

"Where do you think the compass is kept?" Rachel asked.

Gracie walked over to a little table beside the large bed. On it were an oil lamp, a book and a small wooden box.

"Maybe it's in here," she said.

She opened the lid slowly. There was a glow of golden sparkles, and then a tiny fairy sprang out.

Chapter Two
All Wrapped Up

"Hello," said the fairy, landing on the table. "Remember me? I'm Leahann the Birthday Present Fairy."

Leahann had thick, golden blonde hair and big green eyes. She was wearing a swishy blue party dress decorated with yellow stars and stripes.

"Of course we remember you," said
Kirsty, smiling.

Kirsty, Gracie and Khadijah had met
Leahann on their magical adventure with
Niamh the Invitation Fairy. Rachel waved
at the little fairy.

"Hi, I'm Rachel," she said.

"It's lovely to meet you," said Leahann,
waving back at her. "I'm hoping that you
can all help me. You see, a little bird has
told me that the goblins have been using
my magical charm to wrap things."

"What sort of things?" Gracie asked. "You
mean presents?"

"I mean everything," said Leahann. "The
goblins are panicking and making things
worse. I need your help to make them stop.
I know you've been to Goblin Grotto before.
Can you give me any advice? I know I have

to go there, but I'm scared."

"You don't have to go alone," said Khadijah. "We'll go with you."

"Really?" Leahann clapped her hands together. "Oh, thank you!"

She pointed her wand at the compass inside the little wooden box. At once, the compass needle started to whirl around, pointing wildly at all the different directions. A ribbon of shining fairy dust floated out of the compass and wrapped around the girls.

"I can feel my wings growing," said Gracie. "Ooh, that's tickly!"

The captain's cabin seemed to shimmer. The fairy-dust ribbon gently pulled the girls towards the compass. With each step, they grew smaller and smaller, until they were the same size as Leahann. Then, with one last pull, they were inside the compass box. The lid closed, and there was a dazzling flash of light.

"Goblin Grotto!" Rachel exclaimed.

They were fluttering above the goblin village. Snowflakes swirled around them.

"It looks different," said Khadijah.

The usual drab huts had vanished. Instead, the village was a jumble of patterns and bright colours.

"This can't be Goblin Grotto," said Kirsty, turning to Leahann.

"Look closer," Leahann replied.

The fairies swooped downwards and gasped.

"I see it now," said Gracie. "The huts have been gift-wrapped!"

Every goblin home was covered in wrapping paper and tied up with enormous ribbons. They were topped with bows of red, gold, silver and green.

"The village looks like a giant's present table," said Rachel.

"The goblins don't seem very happy about it," Kirsty pointed out.

They could see crowds of goblins stomping up and down the streets. Their squawks carried over the blanket of ice and snow.

"I can't get into my house."

"I tried pushing through the paper but it mended itself."

"I don't like all these awful cheery colours!"

Leahann looked at the goblins running up and down and shook her head.

"My magical charm must be here," she said. "But how can we find the goblin who has it?"

"Don't give up," said Khadijah, slipping

her hand into Leahann's.

"Let's keep flying overhead and watching the goblins," Rachel suggested. "We might spot a clue."

"What does your charm look like?" Gracie asked.

"It's a colourful present wrapped in blue, orange and yellow ribbon," Leahann replied. "You can't miss it."

But the mixture of colours and patterns in the village made it hard to see anything. The fairies flew up and down above streets and alleyways. They looked closely, but no goblins were carrying presents.

"Look down there," said Kirsty. "What do you think they're doing?"

She pointed at a gaggle of goblins in the main square. They had surrounded a single goblin, who was sitting down and shouting at them. The goblins look annoyed.

"Let's find out," said Rachel.

She zoomed down to the square and landed behind the goblins. Her heart was beating fast. The goblins didn't like fairies visiting their home. Kirsty, Leahann, Gracie and Khadijah landed beside her.

"Excuse me," said Rachel in a loud voice.

The goblins jumped and whirled around. The oldest goblin marched up to the fairies and peered into their faces.

"Fairies in Goblin Grotto?" he said. "Good."

"Pardon?" said Rachel, puzzled.

"This is your silly magic," he muttered. "That fool doesn't know how to use it. Teach him and get our village back to normal."

He stomped away, followed by the rest of

the crowd. The only goblin left was the one
sitting down.

"Hang on," said Kirsty, staring at him.
"What's he sitting on?"

The goblin tried
to cover it with his
legs and arms, but
the bright colours
glowed as Leahann
got nearer.

"It's my magical
charm!" she
exclaimed.

"It's not yours; it's
mine," the goblin
shouted. "How does it work?"

"What do you mean?" Kirsty asked,
looking around. "I think you've got it
working very well."

"I was only trying to wrap some presents for myself," said the goblin in a miserable voice. "I said 'wrap everything', and now it won't stop. It'll start wrapping goblins soon."

"You have to give it back," said Khadijah gently. "Leahann can put everything right. After all, it does belong to her."

There was a sudden crack of blue lightning. The fairies stumbled backwards as Jack Frost and Jilly Chilly appeared.

"NO!" Jack Frost yelled. "That charm belongs to me!"

Chapter Three
The Bearers of Bad News

Jack Frost shoved the goblin off the charm and snatched it up.

"My brother and I are going to rule Fairyland," Jilly Chilly boasted.

She leaned towards the fairies. Her spiky hair brushed Leahann's cheek.

"Later, we will attend the Queen's

birthday party," she hissed. "And by the end of the day, I will be queen!"

"Now, get out of here, fairies," Jack Frost said, lacing his long fingers together and giving them a nasty smile. "Tell Titania that I will see her soon."

There was nothing that they could do. Feeling shocked, the five friends fluttered into the air and zoomed away from Goblin Grotto as fast as they could. In silence, they flew towards the Fairyland Palace. Rachel was the first to speak.

"How are we going to tell the Queen that we didn't get the charm?" she asked in a small voice.

"She's going to lose her throne and it's all our fault," said Khadijah.

No one knew what to say. They arrived at the palace feeling miserable. Belle the

Birthday Fairy and Nina the Birthday
Cake Fairy were standing outside. Guests
were already arriving for the party. Rachel
and Kirsty spotted King Arthur and Queen
Grace from the Land of Legends talking to
Charles the Coronation Fairy. Several of
the party fairies waved to them. It would
have been a happy occasion, if only they
had better news.

"Hello!" said Belle as they landed beside
her. "Isn't this exciting?"

"I wish the Queen had delayed the
party," said Leahann in a shaky voice. "We
. . . we didn't get my charm back."

Nina wrapped her in a warm hug.

"The Queen believes in you all," she said.
"She told us to carry on with the party
plan."

"That makes me feel even worse," said

Kirsty, turning away with a groan. "How can we tell her that we have failed?"

"Jack Frost and Jilly Chilly haven't won yet," said Belle encouragingly. "The Queen has faced many challenges over the years, and she has taught us to never give up. There is always a way."

"I wish I could believe that," said Gracie.

"Believe in yourselves," Nina told her. "That's what the Queen does."

"You should go and visit the special

exhibition in the palace gallery," Belle suggested. "It's a celebration of all the things Her Majesty does. Maybe it will help."

Kirsty nodded. At least it would delay them having to tell the Queen that they had failed.

Leahann led them to the Fairyland Palace gallery. The white walls were filled with pictures and portraits of the Queen. Guests were fluttering around, reading the captions and chatting happily. The first wall was labelled 'Everyday Life'. There were pictures of Queen Titania giving new jobs to excited-looking fairies, casting spells to help fairies in need and listening to fairies' concerns.

"Look, here's a picture of the Queen beside the Seeing Pool," said Rachel.

"That's how she watches over Fairyland," said Leahann. "She cares about what's happening in every fairy's life."

Another picture showed the Queen at a desk, writing notes.

"She has many plans for the future of Fairyland," Leahann went on. "She loves finding ways to make our lives even happier."

Khadijah was already looking at the next wall, labelled 'Achievements'. Some of the pictures were hundreds of years old.

She saw the Queen creating new areas of Fairyland, enchanting islands, and designing toadstool houses.

"Is that a dodo with the Queen?" asked Khadijah, peering at a faded photograph.

"Yes," said Leahann, smiling. "Queen Titania invented a complicated magical spell to save extinct animals. If ever an animal becomes extinct in the human world, the species comes to live in Fairyland."

"I really want to meet a dodo," said

Rachel, looking at the picture.

"Oh my goodness," Gracie exclaimed. "We're here!"

Side-by-side photographs of them filled one of the walls. Underneath, the caption said:

One of Queen Titania's greatest achievements was to make some very special human friends. Rachel, Kirsty, Gracie and Khadijah have often helped Fairyland in times of trouble.

Kirsty looked at her friends. She felt a sudden burst of hope.

"We mustn't give up," she said. "If the Queen can do all these things by herself, then together we can beat Jack Frost and Jilly Chilly!"

Chapter Four
A Feast and a Fright

Feeling inspired, the five fairies left the exhibition and went to the ballroom. Long banqueting tables had been arranged around the room, and fairies were sitting on both sides, chattering happily. The King and Queen were at the centre of the top table, surrounded by badly wrapped presents. Balloons bobbed against the ceiling. Gold and silver plates were filled with food, and spices filled the air.

"We've made every fairy's favourite food," said a fairy in a chef's uniform, dashing past them.

The five friends curtsied to the King and Queen.

"Happy Birthday, Your Majesty," said Rachel.

"Thank you, my dear friends," said Queen Titania with a kind smile. "But you look troubled. What is wrong?"

"We haven't got my charm back," said

Leahann, hanging her head. "I'm sorry, Your Majesty. I've let you down."

"Jack Frost and Jilly Chilly will be here soon," Gracie added.

The Queen raised her hand to stop them and spoke in a calm tone. "Please try not to worry. I have been on the throne for many years, and I have seen that good always wins in the end. Let go of your fears and trust in the magic."

"And in the meantime," added King Oberon. "Feast!"

They found some empty chairs and took their places at the table. Rachel looked

around in wonder.

"I think this is the biggest banquet I've ever seen in Fairyland," she said.

"I can see every single fairy we've ever met," Kirsty whispered. "And lots more that we don't yet know."

"How can every fairy fit into one ballroom?" asked Khadijah.

"The Queen enchanted the room for the party," Leahann explained. "It will expand to fit the number of guests."

The food was so delicious that everyone forgot about the missing charm. The fairy chef had worked very hard to make everyone's favourite food.

"That's her magical gift," Leahann explained to the others. "She knows what everyone in Fairyland likes best to eat."

The dishes were passed around the

tables so that everyone could have a taste.
There were fragrant curries with delicate,
jasmine-scented rice, golden-crusted pies,
fluffy potato puffs and salty seaweed crisps.
Perfectly ripe fruits spilled from bowls,
from blush-pink grapes and freshly picked
strawberries to
soft, plump figs
and ruby-red
watermelon.

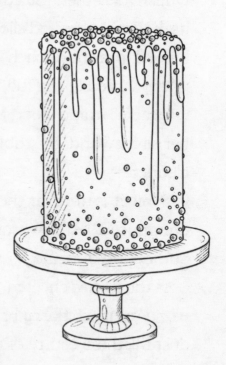

"I couldn't eat
another bite," said
Khadijah.

Nina smiled
and waved her
wand. A huge cake
appeared in the
centre of the room,
frosted with white

icing and sprinkled with tiny silver balls.

"Are you sure you can't manage any more?" Gracie asked Khadijah with a smile.

"There is always room for cake," said Khadijah, laughing.

They all sang 'Happy Birthday' to the Queen, and then the cake magically cut itself. Perfectly sized slices floated out and landed in front of each guest.

"Now I really am full," said Khadijah.

Queen Titania stood up. With a wave of her silver wand, the tables were cleared and cleaned.

"Now it is time for the ceremony," she announced. "Afterwards, there will be games and dancing."

As the fairies cheered, she waved her wand again. A flurry of sparkling fairy dust filled the centre of the room. When it cleared, her throne had appeared. Charles the Coronation Fairy flew out of his seat and stood beside it.

"He's performing the ceremony," Leahann whispered.

Charles opened his mouth to speak . . .

CRASH! The ballroom doors flew open and an icy blast of wind rushed in. *CRACK!* With a flash of blue lightning, a tall, bony figure appeared in the ballroom doorway. A grey mist swirled into the room, and everyone shivered.

"It's Jack Frost," Gracie exclaimed.
"We've run out of time!"

Chapter Five
Pickpocket!

Jack Frost had Leahann's magical birthday charm in his hands. His cloak billowed in the freezing wind, and tiny icicles dropped from his beard and smashed on the floor.

"It's time for you to admit defeat," he told Queen Titania.

His voice crackled with anger.

Jilly Chilly stepped out from behind her brother's cloak. She patted his arm with her icy hand.

"Don't be angry, dear brother," she hissed. "This is a celebration. It is time for us to rule Fairyland."

"Never!" shouted a very young fairy from the back of the room.

"None of you can stop me," said Jack Frost. "I've been reading Fairyland law. Your queen can't renew her right to the throne without all the charms. Isn't that true, Your Majesty?"

"That is quite true," Queen Titania agreed.

She was pale but fearless.

"Fairyland law allows me to claim the throne if the Queen doesn't carry out the ceremony," Jilly Chilly added. "I therefore

claim the right to be queen and make my
brother the king."

There was a horrified silence. Then,
looking at the brother and sister side by
side, Rachel had an idea.

"Jack Frost and Jilly Chilly often annoy
each other," she whispered to the others.
"What if we could make them squabble?
They might be so distracted that we could
get the charm back before they notice."

She stood up and looked at Jilly Chilly.

"Why do you get to be the ruler?" she
asked. "I thought Jack Frost wanted to be in
charge."

"We'll both be rulers but I will be in
charge," Jack Frost growled under his
breath.

"Oh no you won't," said Jilly Chilly,
turning to glare at him. "I'm going to be top

ruler. I'll boss you around."

"Kings are better than queens," Jack Frost snapped.

"Rubbish," Jilly Chilly retorted. "Give me my charm."

"It's mine," said Jack Frost. "I stole it, I own it."

Jilly Chilly snatched at the magical birthday present, but Jack Frost hid it under his cloak.

"Give it back," she yelled at her brother. "I have to hold it for the magic to make me queen."

"Tough luck," Jack Frost yelled back at her. "I'll be top ruler."

He stormed out of the room and Rachel sprang to her feet.

"We have to follow him," she whispered to the others. "It's up to us to get that charm."

They zoomed past Jilly Chilly, who had wrapped her cloak around her. Jack Frost was already halfway up the grand staircase. The fairies flew over his head and landed on the steps above him.

"This is my home now," he told them. "Get out!"

"This will never be your home," said Kirsty. "Give the charm back."

"Charm?" Jack Frost said in a sing-song, mocking voice. "What charm?"

He held out empty hands and smiled unpleasantly.

"We know you have it under your cloak," said Khadijah.

Jack Frost's fingertips crackled with blue electricity. He reached inside his cloak and pulled out a half-eaten bogmallow.

"You mean this?" he asked.

"You know what we mean," Rachel said quietly.

Jack Frost threw the bogmallow down the stairs and cackled with laughter.

"You mean this?" he asked, reaching inside his cloak again.

His smile faded. He felt around inside his

cloak. Then his face went red with anger.

"That cheat has picked my pocket!" he yelled. "Sisters are the worst!"

He ran helter skelter down the stairs and skidded into the ballroom doorway. The fairies zoomed in behind him.

"No!" cried Gracie.

Beside the throne, Queen Titania was taking off her crown. Jilly Chilly was smiling and holding the birthday present charm in her hands.

"We are here today to give Fairyland a new queen," said

Charles the Coronation Fairy in a miserable voice. "A new chapter of history is about to begin."

Chapter Six
Fairyland's Queen

Suddenly, all around the ballroom, chairs scraped on the polished floor. All the fairies had stood up.

"No," said Samira the Superhero Fairy.

"No," called out the Rainbow Fairies.

"No, no, no," rang out the fairy voices.

One by one, each guest flew forward and

stood between Jilly Chilly and the throne. Soon, they had hidden it from her view. Jilly Chilly glared at them.

"It doesn't matter what you do," she sneered. "You cannot break ancient Fairyland laws."

Kirsty looked at the Queen. She was standing very still with her crown in her hands. She would not work against the laws of Fairyland. No one knew them better than Queen Titania.

"That's it!" Kirsty said with a gasp.

Her mind whirled. Suddenly she knew exactly how to stop Jilly Chilly. She flew forward and landed in front of Jack Frost's sister.

"All right," she said. "You're going to be queen. Do you know what the Queen of Fairyland does all day?"

"Sits on her throne while servants wait on her," said Jilly Chilly in a confident voice.

"There's a bit more to it than that," said Kirsty, thinking back to the exhibition in the palace gallery. "Let me think. You will have to watch over every fairy in the Seeing Pool and make sure that you are there to help them with their problems. You will have a lot of reading to do. After all, there are books filled with the laws of Fairyland and you need to know them all by heart. That's a lot of studying."

"I hate reading," said Jilly Chilly. "I won't do it."

"Fairyland will crumble if you don't," said Queen Titania. "There will be nothing to rule."

"You will have to design and create brand-new lands whenever they are needed," added Rachel, who had realised what Kirsty was doing.

"Yes," said Khadijah, "and you will have to guess what Fairyland will need over the next few years and be prepared for the unexpected."

Jilly Chilly had stopped smiling.

"Don't listen to them," Jack Frost shouted.

"Create new spells to connect with the human world," Gracie went on.

"Build good friendships with the other magical creatures who share the land," Kirsty continued. "Know when to ask for help."

"Learn about and understand all the human beliefs and festivals," added Elisha the Eid Fairy.

"There's much more," said Kirsty. "It's all listed in the gallery. "The Queen never stops working."

Jilly Chilly's face was like thunder. She turned to Jack Frost, and her mouth twisted into a scowl.

"You tried to trick me," she hissed. "You were going to make me do all that hard work. You lazy frozen beanpole!"

"But . . ."

"I'm not wasting my time doing all that rubbish," she yelled. "I'll never listen to you again!"

She flung the birthday present charm at Leahann and stormed out of the ballroom. With a wail of rage, Jack Frost followed her. The grey mist melted away, and the sun gleamed through the ballroom windows. A great cheer went up from all the fairies.

"You did it!" Leahann exclaimed, hugging Kirsty, Rachel, Gracie and Khadijah. "You're amazing."

"It wasn't us who saved the day," said Kirsty. "It was Queen Titania and all her hard work."

Together, the fairies curtsied and bowed to their queen. Charles the Coronation Fairy gently took her crown and placed it back on her head. Tears of happiness twinkled in her eyes.

"I call upon the Birthday Party Fairies to step forward with their charms," Charles announced.

Niamh, Sara, Lois and Leahann stood in a semicircle around the throne, holding

their magical objects. Queen Titania sat in her throne, and the invitation, the hat, the balloons and the magical present glowed in the royal colours of purple and gold. Fairy dust rose up from them and made the crown glow too.

"By this ancient fairy magic, we renew you as Queen of Fairyland," said Charles in a loud voice. "Long live the Queen!"

Everyone cheered and clapped. Laughing, Queen Titania rose to her feet and waved her wand. The tables and chairs vanished away, and a stage appeared at the end of the ballroom.

"Thank you all," she said. "It is a great honour and a joy to be your queen. Now we can celebrate with magical music and dancing!"

The Music Fairies flew up on stage with

Destiny the Pop Star Fairy and Jae the Boy Band Fairy. Soon the ballroom was filled with dancing fairies. Queen Titania turned to Rachel, Kirsty, Gracie and Khadijah.

"Once again you have shown me that you are true friends of Fairyland," she said. "Thank you for all you have done. Because of you, Fairyland's future is sparkling!"

"We were happy to help, Your Majesty," said Kirsty.

The Queen gave them a beautiful smile. Then King Oberon took her hand.

"May I have this dance?" he asked, his eyes twinkling.

The King and Queen danced away in each other's arms.

"A perfect end to a perfect party," said Leahann. "And all the presents are perfect too. Thank you for helping us to make this the best birthday ever."

"Talking of presents," said Kirsty, "I know that Gracie has some gifts to open. Maybe we should be getting back to the pirate ship."

"Yes," said Rachel. "After all, we have a treasure hunt to finish."

Leahann raised her wand. In a trice, the four friends were surrounded by a whirl of glittering fairy dust. Their wings melted away and they felt themselves returning to human size. Then, with four gentle bumps, they landed back in the captain's cabin. Not a moment had passed since they left.

"I've just realised," said Khadijah. "This means we get two birthday feasts."

"Two birthday cakes," Kirsty added.

"This must be our lucky day," said Rachel.

"Leahann was right," Gracie agreed.
"Best birthday ever!"

The End

**Join Kirsty and Rachel on two
winter adventures in the . . .**

Winter Wishes Collection

Read on for a sneak peek . . .

"We're going to try out the snow," Kirsty
Tate called to her mum. "We'll be back for
lunch, OK?"

"See you later!" Rachel Walker shouted to
her mum and dad.

The two friends grinned at each other
as their parents called back goodbyes.
Both girls were wearing new salopettes,
puffa jackets, woolly hats and gloves.
Kirsty pushed open the door of the chalet,
and out they stepped, blinking in the bright
sunshine.

Mountain peaks rose majestically
all around, covered in thick white snow.

Skiers were already whizzing down the slopes, zig-zagging across the mountainside in colourful groups. Other people were careering about on snowboards, sun glinting off their snow goggles.

Rachel couldn't stop smiling. "It's so fantastic being on holiday with you again!" she said happily.

Kirsty nodded. "I know," she said, linking arms with her best friend. "All this snow, and the Winter Festival in a few days to look forward to, as well." She beamed. "And you never know, we might meet a fairy, too. We always have such magical adventures when we're together!"

The girls' parents had rented them skis and a snowboard each, and Rachel and Kirsty went to find them in the small shed at the side of the chalet. "I'm going to try

my skis first," Kirsty decided, taking a pair
of ski poles, skis and special ski boots. She
sat down to put them on, feeling tingly with
excitement.

"I'll try a snowboard," Rachel said
eagerly, picking up a turquoise board that
was long and slender, with rounded ends.

Once they were both ready, they
found a small slope to practise on.

"Wheeee!" Kirsty squealed, pushing off.
"Here I go!" She whizzed down the slope,
but wobbled at the end and fell sideways
into the snow. Ouch! It was hard and icy.
She got to her feet gingerly, rubbing her
legs.

"My turn now . . . Wheeee!" cried Rachel,
standing on her board and riding downhill
on it. It was hard keeping her balance,
though, and she fell off too. "Ow!" she cried,

as her elbow bumped on a particularly hard patch of ice. "This snow isn't very soft, is it?"

Kirsty shook her head. "Look at that girl over there," she murmured, helping her friend up. "The snow's so hard, she can't even build her snowman!"

Rachel watched the girl, who was struggling with her snowman nearby. The snow wasn't clumping together properly, and crumbled to ice chips instead.

"Maybe we should leave skiing and snowboarding for a bit later," Rachel suggested. "How about a snowball fight?"

"You're on," Kirsty laughed, quickly unstrapping her skis.

The girls started making snowballs but the snow didn't stick together very well. And then, when they started throwing them at one another, the snowballs were so hard, they really hurt!

Rachel had just opened her mouth to suggest they try something else when she saw a snowball zooming towards her face. Before she could duck, the snowball suddenly burst apart in a puff of sparkling snow crystals. Rachel jumped in surprise . . . and then stared as she noticed a little fairy hovering in mid-air, right where the snowball had been.

"Oh!" gasped Rachel in surprise. "Hello! Who are you?"

The fairy had chestnut-brown hair with a fringe and wore fluffy white earmuffs tipped with silver glitter. She was dressed in a purple coat with a red-and-purple striped dress underneath, red leggings and purple snow boots.

"I'm Gabriella," the fairy said, dropping a dainty curtsey. "Gabriella the Snow Kingdom Fairy. And I'm really glad to see you here!"

Kirsty came over excitedly. "Hi, Gabriella," she said to the tiny fairy. "I'm Kirsty. Is everything all right?"

Gabriella shook her head sadly. "No," she said. "Jack Frost is up to his tricks again! He's stolen my special Magic Snowflake, which makes all the snow soft, fluffy and white. Without it, the snow everywhere is much harder and icier."

"We noticed," Kirsty said. "How did he get your snowflake?"

"Well, every year on the first of December, I hang my Magic Snowflake on the Christmas Tree outside the Fairyland palace," Gabriella explained. "But this morning the snowflake was gone – and there were goblin footprints all around the tree. I'm sure Jack Frost ordered his goblins to steal it, and hide it in the human world."

"We'll help you look for it," Rachel said at once.

"Thank you," Gabriella said gratefully. "It'll be difficult to spot, I'm afraid. The only clue will be if we see any snow that looks perfectly sparkly and fluffy. That could mean my Magic Snowflake is nearby."

Kirsty gazed around . . . then frowned as she noticed that it was snowing over a nearby pine forest. "How weird," she commented. "It's snowing there – but not here!"

Gabriella swung round to see, her head tilted as she looked carefully at the falling flakes. Then a smile appeared on her face. "They look like proper snowflakes to me," she declared.

"Does that mean . . . ?" Rachel began excitedly.

Gabriella nodded. "Yes," she said. "I'm sure my Magic Snowflake must be in that forest. Let's go and look!"

Read the Winter Wishes Collection to find out what adventures are in store for Kirsty and Rachel!

RAINBOW magic™

Calling all parents, carers and teachers!

The Rainbow Magic fairies are here to help
your child enter the magical world of reading.
Whatever reading stage they are at, there's
a Rainbow Magic book for everyone!
Here is Lydia the Reading Fairy's guide to
supporting your child's journey at all levels.

1

Starting Out

Our Rainbow Magic Beginner Readers are perfect for first-time readers who are just beginning to develop reading skills and confidence. Approved by teachers, they contain a full range of educational levelling, as well as lively full-colour illustrations.

2

Developing Readers

Rainbow Magic Early Readers contain longer stories and wider vocabulary for building stamina and growing confidence. These are adaptations of our most popular Rainbow Magic stories, specially developed for younger readers in conjunction with an Early Years reading consultant, with full-colour illustrations.

3

Going Solo

The Rainbow Magic chapter books – a mixture of series and one-off specials – contain accessible writing to encourage your child to venture into reading independently. These highly collectible and much-loved magical stories inspire a love of reading to last a lifetime.

www.orchardseriesbooks.co.uk

"Rainbow Magic got my daughter reading chapter books. Great sparkly covers, cute fairies and traditional stories full of magic that she found impossible to put down" – Mother of Edie (6 years)

"Florence LOVES the Rainbow Magic books.
She really enjoys reading now"
– Mother of Florence (6 years)

Read along the Reading Rainbow!

Well done - you have completed the book!

This book was worth 1 star

See how far you have climbed on the Reading Rainbow opposite.
The more books you read, the more stars you can colour in
and the closer you will be to becoming a Royal Fairy!

Do you want to print your own Reading Rainbow?

1. Go to the Rainbow Magic website

2. Download and print out the poster

3. Colour in a star for every book you finish and climb the Reading Rainbow

4. For every step up the rainbow, you can download your very own certificate.

There's all this and lots more at
orchardseriesbooks.co.uk

You'll find activities, stories, a special newsletter AND you can
search for the fairy with your name!